Busytown Mysteries™

With the timeless characters of RICHARD SCARRY

The Pizza Delivery Mystery

adapted by Natalie Shaw
based on the screenplay
written by Bob Ardiel

Simon Spotlight
New York   London   Toronto   Sydney

SIMON SPOTLIGHT
An imprint of Simon & Schuster Children's Publishing Division
1230 Avenue of the Americas, New York, New York 10020
Busytown Mysteries™ and all related and associated trademarks are owned by Cookie Jar Entertainment Inc.
and used under license from Cookie Jar Entertainment Inc. © 2011 Cookie Jar Entertainment Inc. All rights
reserved. All rights reserved, including the right of reproduction in whole or in part in any form.
SIMON SPOTLIGHT and colophon are registered trademarks of Simon & Schuster, Inc.
For information about special discounts for bulk purchases, please contact Simon & Schuster Special Sales
at 1-866-506-1949 or business@simonandschuster.com.
Manufactured in the United States of America 0911 LAK
First Edition 10 9 8 7 6 5 4 3 2 1
ISBN 978-1-4424-2699-3

It was lunchtime in Busytown, and Huckle, Sally, and Lowly were *mighty* hungry. They had been waiting for over an hour for Peppino to deliver the pizza they had ordered. Lowly's stomach was growling so loud he could hear it through his headphones!

"Since Peppino doesn't seem to be coming to us, maybe we should go to Peppino's!" said Lowly.

At Peppino's Pizzeria, they found Pig Will and Pig Won't sitting at a table.

"Hi, Pig Will! Hi, Pig Won't! Have you seen Peppino?" asked Huckle.

"Hi, Huckle!" replied Pig Will. "He went out to deliver some pizzas, but he never came back."

"We're hungry!" shouted Pig Won't. "What's taking him so long?"

"That's a good question!" said Huckle. "I think we have a mystery!"

Just then the Busytown Action Bug News van drove inside.

The roof of the news van slid open, and Goldbug popped out.

"*Mamma mia!* We have a pizza problem!" said Goldbug. "Can Huckle and his team find Peppino and solve the Pizza Delivery Mystery?"

Huckle started to look for clues in the pizzeria. He noticed that the pizza oven was warm but empty. Peppino must have finished baking his pizzas and left to deliver them. But to whom?

"Look, another clue!" Lowly called out, showing an order slip to Huckle. "It says Bruno Bear and Mr. Souza ordered pizza, and your name is at the end. Let's see if Peppino made it to the first delivery stop. To Bruno Bear's house!"

They knocked on Bruno Bear's door. "Hi, kids!" Bruno said, holding a slice of pizza. "What can I do for you?"

"Well we wanted to ask you a question, but you've already answered it," Huckle said.

"I have?" Bruno wondered aloud. "In that case, would you like some pizza?"

"Thanks, Bruno, but we have a mystery to solve," said Huckle. "Next stop: Mr. Souza's!"

They arrived at Mr. Souza's building. Mr. Souza's music school was on the top floor, so Sally pressed the elevator button.

"Did you know Mr. Souza is Hilda Hippo's music teacher?" asked Lowly. "I wonder if he could teach *me* to play the tuba! Ha-ha!"

Sally sniffed the air. "Do any of you smell pizza?" she asked.

"I can *smell* pizza, but I can't *see* it!" answered Huckle. "Maybe we're so hungry we're imagining it!"

Sally pressed the elevator button again, but nothing happened.

"I wonder if this elevator is broken," she said. "The light doesn't even work!"

That gave Huckle an idea. If they couldn't get up to Mr. Souza's, they could try calling him on the phone! They all ran outside to find a telephone booth.

Huckle called Mr. Souza. "Hi, Mr. Souza, this is Huckle Cat," he said. "I was wondering if Peppino delivered a pizza to you today?"

"That's funny," answered Mr. Souza. "I've been waiting for Peppino for over an hour. And I'm waiting for Hilda, too! She was supposed to come in for a music lesson. Have you seen her?"

"I haven't," said Huckle, "but I'll let you know if I do. Oh, and I think your elevator is broken!" Huckle thanked Mr. Souza and hung up the phone.

They walked back to Mr. Souza's building through the parking lot.
"Hey, look, guys!" Sally said. "Isn't that Peppino's truck?"
Lowly did a double take. "Yes! And isn't that Hilda's car over there?"
"You're right!" said Huckle. "But where are Peppino and Hilda?"

"They have to be somewhere between their cars and Mr. Souza's music school!" said Lowly.

"Wait! Isn't the elevator broken?" said Huckle. "I think I may have solved the mystery!"

Just then the Busytown Action News van drove in, and Goldbug popped out. "Did you find out what happened to Peppino and your pizza, Huckle?" he asked.

"Yup! Here's what I think happened," said Huckle. "We could smell pizza in the building but couldn't go up to Mr. Souza's because the elevator was broken. Peppino never delivered Mr. Souza's pizza and Hilda never arrived for her lesson, yet both of their cars are parked outside! So I think that both Peppino and Hilda are stuck in the broken elevator!"

Just then an elevator repairman arrived. "Mr. Souza called me to repair the elevator," he said.

"Please hurry," said Sally. "We think our friends are stuck inside!"

"Oh dear!" said the repairman. He looked closely at the elevator button. "Aha! It looks like a wire was loose. Let's see if it works now."

After he tightened the wire the elevator button lit up!

The elevator doors slid open. Peppino and Hilda were inside!

"Yay!" shouted Hilda. "You saved us!"

"It must have been awful to be stuck inside that broken elevator," Sally said.

"Well not when you have some good music to listen to," replied Peppino.

"And delicious pizza to eat!"
added Hilda.

They got so hungry while they
were waiting in the elevator that
they ate *both* Mr. Souza's and
Huckle's pizzas!

"Don't worry!" said Peppino. "I
promise to bake new ones!"

When they returned to Peppino's Pizzeria it
was a big mess!

"Oh, no!" said Huckle. "What happened?"

"We were tired of waiting, so we tried to make
a pizza ourselves," said Pig Will.

"We were going to call it the Pig Will and Pig Won't Double-Deluxe Extreme-Supreme Pizza!" added Pig Won't.

"Hmmm. I'd call it the Pig Will and Pig Won't Double-Trouble Disaster Pizza!" said Lowly, making everyone laugh.

The kids all helped to tidy up the pizzeria.

After Peppino made more pizzas to thank everyone for solving the mystery, he left to make one last delivery.

"Where did Peppino go now?" Sally asked.

"Why, to deliver a *new* pizza to Mr. Souza like he promised!" said Huckle. "Mr. Souza must be starving!"